TRINITY
COLLEGE LONDON PRESS

GW00689574

GRADE **01**

PIANO

**12 pieces plus exercises for
Trinity College London
exams 2021-2023**

Now with performance notes

Published by
Trinity College London Press Ltd
trinitycollege.com

Registered in England
Company no. 09726123

Copyright © 2020 Trinity College London Press Ltd
First impression, June 2020

Cover photograph courtesy of Steinway & Sons

Printed in England by Caligraving Ltd

Performance notes

King William's March / Clarke   Page 5

- Baroque
- Shifts of hand position
- Legato and staccato playing

The King William mentioned in the title of this piece, is William of Orange, who became King of England in 1689. As you'd expect for a march written for a king, it is stately and majestic.

Although we're playing it on the piano, imagine this played on a trumpet, perhaps as a fanfare for the arrival of King William. The *staccato* opening helps to give a clear sense of rhythm and this follows into the *legato* quavers too, which you might like to think of as quite deliberate and important – they're certainly not in a hurry! There are also some large intervals in this piece in both hands, which need careful negotiation, particularly when the hand position changes as well. The right-hand shifts in bars 2 and 6 are good examples, and it's worth thinking about shortening the first note of these bars slightly to give you the time you need to move. It's better that way than risking any danger of being late for the next note and interrupting the march rhythm.

Jeremiah Clarke's most famous piece is the 'Prince of Denmark's March', which is very similar in style to 'King William's March'. See if you can find a recording for solo trumpet, perhaps with organ accompaniment, to give you a sense of the majestic style of this music.

Passepied in C major / Handel   Page 6

- Baroque
- Upbeats
- Dialogue between the hands

A *Passepied* is a dance movement, with the title translating literally as 'pass-foot'. Originally a lively folk dance from Brittany, by Handel's day it had become a more refined courtly dance.

As with all Passepieds, this piece begins with an upbeat and each time you come across another one, (at the end of bars 2, 6, 8 and 10), it might be useful to think of them like a springboard, lifting you onto the first beat of the next bar. This fits nicely with the dance feel – the upbeats are perhaps where you have a foot in the air (or crossed over, as in the original Passepied dance), and the downbeats are where both feet are on the floor. You could try it out yourself! Notice that where the upbeat and downbeat are on the same pitch in the second half of the piece, the suggested fingering is different for the two notes, to help give that lifted and buoyant effect.

The second half of the piece also contains some 'conversation' between the hands, with the right-hand melody in bar 7 copied by the left hand in bar 8, and then the same effect happens again in bars 9 and 10. The second time, the notes in both hands have moved up (an ascending sequence), and this helpfully coincides with the *crescendo* marking – you might like to think of the conversation between the hands becoming slightly more argumentative at this point!

It would be worth listening to some other dance movements by Handel when you are learning this piece: try a movement or two from the *Music for the Royal Fireworks* or the *Water Music*, some of his most famous compositions.

Arioso / Türk   Page 7

- Classical
- Projection of right-hand melody
- Phrasing

'Arioso' refers to a piece that is vocal in style – written in a similar way to a song. In this piece, you might like to think of the right hand as a singer, with its beautiful and expressive melody.

Although the right hand takes the lead, it's important not to neglect the left hand too much – for example, when there are long rests in the second and fourth lines make sure that you're prepared early for the left hand to come back in. You want to avoid a last-second scramble to find the right note!

It's also worth spending a bit of time thinking about the ends of phrases in this piece. Except for the very end of the piece, each phrase finishes with two slurred notes – aim for the first one to be slightly emphasised, and the second one to be softer. This fits in well with each phrase being rather like an arch, getting a little louder as you approach the middle, and then gradually softening as you get to the end. It's often helpful to think of phrases as musical sentences – you could try to pinpoint the most important note in each phrase, as you might highlight an important word in a sentence.

Perhaps the most well-known Arioso is by Johann Sebastian Bach, from *Cantata 156*. Have a listen and see what similarities you can hear.

Donkey Trot / Holland   Page 8

- Character piece
- Variety of articulation
- Use of sustaining pedal

The 'donkey's trot' in this piece can be heard in the left hand, and is on the go for most of the piece. Once the trotting finishes near the end, you might like to think of the last two chords as a distant echo of a donkey's 'hee-haw'.

At the beginning, it's a good idea to write a reminder to put your foot on the sustaining pedal, just so you're ready for when it's needed, even though that's not until the last four bars of the piece! It's also perhaps worth thinking ahead to the hardest part of the piece – maybe bars 17-18 – so that you have that in mind when setting the tempo at the opening. The indication 'non legato' applies mostly to the left hand, and means the notes can be slightly separated, although not as much as staccato. There are plenty of different articulations and playing indications, and it really brings the piece to life if you can incorporate these. In the right hand in first bar, you might like to think of springing lightly up off the first note (staccato) and then landing a little more firmly on the second note to give it the slight emphasis that's marked.

Bars 14-16 have an unusual combination of dynamics marked, and it's probably easiest to think of each of these bars starting progressively louder, but with the end of each bar slightly softer than the start. In bars 17-18, the left hand jumps up to play the E flat in the chord. The different directions of the stems indicate that both hands are involved, so the three notes go down together, despite looking a little separated on the page.

For a rather more energetic donkey, definitely galloping not trotting, have a listen to 'Wild Donkeys' from Camille Saint-Saëns' Carnival of the Animals. The donkeys gallop so fast that the piece is less than a minute long!

Walking Together / Norton   Page 9

- Equality between both hands
- Long, flowing phrases
- Expressive dynamics

'Walking Together' comes from Christopher Norton's Microjazz series which covers many instruments. These pieces blend together lots of different musical styles, including Classical, Jazz, Rock and Pop.

According to the composer, the performer should aim for 'absolute togetherness' with this piece. You might want to play this towards the higher end of the given tempo range, which will help achieve the sense of flow and moving together.

The left hand should take the reins of the melody into bar 9, as the right hand accompanies with a short, punchy rhythm. Making the most of the crescendo in bar 8 will make this exchange more obvious.

Have a listen to Christopher Norton's other pieces – he has his own YouTube channel.

Last Waltz (duet) / Terzibaschitsch   Page 10

- Melody and accompaniment over four hands
- Candidate part spans both hands
- Both performers share the lead

The Waltz is a very famous dance style between two people. This piece therefore has a dance-like feel to it, with the distinctive 'um-pah-pah' rhythm common to every waltz.

'Last Waltz' has a slightly sad quality to it, being in a minor key. Perhaps this is about two people sharing a last dance before departing and not seeing each other for a long time. Performers could therefore emphasise the romantic, expressive parts of this duet, especially the rising and

falling in dynamics in bars 3-4 and bars 11-12. You may wish to be generous with these crescendos and diminuendos, and paying attention to them in this way will help bring a yearning quality.

Let the duet part take over during bars 17-24, where they have the melody, while the candidate 'poms' away with short chords. You will need to listen carefully to the duet part, especially when the music slows down over bars 23-24, before you take the lead again in bar 25. The music gets slower over the final two bars, but you get to decide how slow it gets. Slowing down gradually will help paint the picture of this sad dance.

Stealth Mode / Bober   Page 12

- Crossing hands
- Staccato
- Switching clefs in the left hand

Like many of Melody Bober's pieces, 'Stealth Mode' introduces certain techniques of piano playing. This piece features sneaky, short notes and sleight of the (left) hand!

The short, staccato notes are important in making this piece sound stealthy – perhaps you could play as though you are walking on tip-toe... Although there are no indicated changes in dynamic within the phrases, you may wish to accentuate the rise and fall of each line, as though someone is sneaking around and then hiding out of sight once again. Just like the music, the performer can become stealthy when the left hand crosses over to reach the top notes. In the first line, for example, once the left hand has played the first chord, it is a good idea to prepare the new position of the left hand as early as possible, while the right hand keeps its position. Preparing the left hand in this way throughout will help make this music sound sneaky.

Pirate Stomp / Yandell   Page 14

- Fast tempo
- Accelerando
- Sea shanty style

Avast ye! 'Pirate Stomp' is classic 'Piratey' music much like 'The Drunken Sailor' or 'The Pirates of the Caribbean'. The strong sense of rhythm in sea shanties like these came from the need for sailors to pull together when working aboard ship.

Just like all work songs, this piece has a strong first beat of each bar, so you can emphasise this to create the energetic sound of a rowdy group of pirates stomping around on their ship. The last two bars get faster and race towards an exciting 'Hey!' on the very last note. It is a good idea to work out your beginning tempo to take account of the faster tempo that will be needed at the end.

Bar 17 features a 'sneaky' pause just before this exciting finish. You might want to experiment with how long you hold the last note in bar 17, making the ending as surprising and mischievous as possible!

As this piece is fast, it is a good idea to keep the right-hand position the same for each phrase and use all the fingers. For example, over bars 3-4, you could use fingers 1, 3, 4 and 5.

Try playing other pirate music such as 'The Drunken Sailor' – you could try to play it by ear as it is similar to 'Pirate Stomp'.

The Croc That Swallowed a Clock / Tanner   Page 15

▶ Counting and rhythm
▶ Sustained notes
▶ Character

Mark Tanner composes a wide variety of highly attractive music for piano students of all levels, and this appealing piece is no exception. The story of the crocodile that swallowed a clock comes from J M Barrie's *Peter Pan*, the ticking a helpful warning that the beast is approaching!

This music is bursting with character, the tick of the clock (and perhaps also the snap of the crocodile's jaws) colourfully portrayed in *staccato* notes/chords in both hands. Make your *staccato* crisp and rhythmic, and absolutely in time. You might find a metronome helpful here – it will certainly give you a good sense of the ticking clock! The tied semibreves in bars 2, 5 and 13 are easy to sustain with good fingering, leaving other fingers free to play the chords.

By the time we reach bar 7, the ticking has been replaced by long smooth notes, suggesting the crocodile sliding about as it gets closer. Make the slurred minims really smooth here to contrast with the earlier *staccato* notes. In the final bars, the crocodile seems to be retreating only to reappear with a ff accented semibreve and a final dramatic cluster chord in the left hand to be played with a sharp snap of sound!

Space Walk Rag / Hawthorn & Suschitzky   Page 16

▶ Contemporary ragtime
▶ Rhythm
▶ Hand independence

A Rag is a jazzy piece of music usually in duple time with a strict left-hand beat and a bouncy syncopated (off beat) right-hand melody. The most famous piano rags were composed by Scott Joplin – listen to his 'Maple Leaf Rag' to hear the distinctive style, syncopated rhythms and unexpected harmonies.

Just as in a traditional rag, in 'Space Walk Rag' the left hand marks the beat while the right hand plays a catchy syncopated melody, characterised by contrasting slurred (*legato*) and *staccato* notes. Don't be tempted to 'swing' the quavers, especially in bars 3, 7 and 15 as the swinging character of the music comes from the tied notes. Count carefully throughout and practise hands separately to ensure the left-hand beat is secure and the right-hand melody notes come in at the right time, especially the off-beat quavers in bars 1, 5, 9 and 13. Good staccato will enhance the jaunty character of the music – bounce the hand and wrist out of the keyboard to create a clean, crisp sound. Although marked *mf*, experiment with changes in the dynamics to bring even greater character to the music.

The Very Vicious Velociraptor / Hall & Drayton   Page 17

▶ Hand coordination
▶ Articulation
▶ Characterisation and expression

This delightful piece is sure to capture the imagination of children who will enjoy its imagery and the chance to bring drama and expression to the music.

A velociraptor was a small, fast-moving dinosaur with crocodile-like jaws and sharp claws, characteristics which are brilliantly illustrated in the music. The quaver phrases suggest speed while the accented *staccato* chords represent vicious teeth and claws!

The quaver sequence from bars 12-14 should be shared between the hands with an accent on the first note of each grouping. To keep this section flowing and dramatic, practise moving the hands into the new position for each bar as soon as one hand has finished its run of notes – for example, the right hand will hover over the left-hand position in bar 12 in preparation for the next run of notes beginning on B in bar 13.

The drama of this piece comes largely from the contrasting articulation – the *legato* quaver figures suggest not only the speed of the dinosaur but also a sense of concern, while the *staccato* notes are the snap of its jaws. The dynamics fade towards the end, perhaps indicating that the velociraptor has retreated to its lair!

Viking Village / Pittarello   Page 18

▶ Accidentals
▶ Intervals
▶ Rhythm

A circle of huts and Vikings huddled around their campfire is evoked in this characterful piece by young composer Matthew Pittarello. A sense of menace is suggested by the accidentals, and the 5ths in the left hand in bars 5-6. The notes lie comfortably under the hands in a five-finger position and the scale patterns in bars 11 and 13 should be easy to manage.

Control of dynamics is important in creating atmosphere, from the haunting off-beat horn call of bars 1 and 3, which is a repeating motif in the piece, to the hairpins in bars 11-14, and the *crescendo* in bars 15-16, whose chords and rhythm suggest drums. Aim for plenty of drama to bring the story of the music to life and give the final *staccato* note in the left hand a brisk strike with either the second or third finger to highlight the *sf*.

Authors: Martin Ford, Owen Barton and Frances Wilson

King William's March

Jeremiah Clarke
(c.1674-1707)

Passepied in C major

HWV 559

George Frideric Handel (1685-1759)

ed. Peter Wild

Moderato ♩ = 104

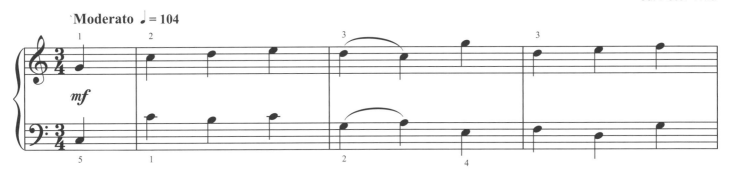

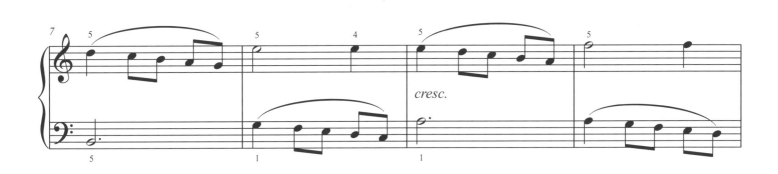

Omit the repeats in the exam.

Arioso

from *Klavierschüle*

Daniel Gottlob Türk
(1756–1813)

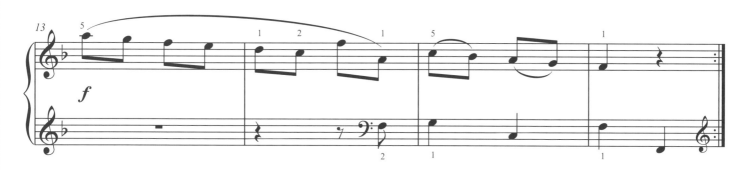

Omit the repeats in the exam.

Donkey Trot

Dulcie Holland
(1913-2000)

Walking Together

Christopher Norton
(b. 1953)

Composer's metronome mark ♩. = *c.* **60**

Last Waltz

(duet part)

Anne Terzibaschitsch
(b. 1955)

Last Waltz

(candidate's part)

Anne Terzibaschitsch
(b. 1955)

Stealth Mode

Melody Bober
(b. 1955)

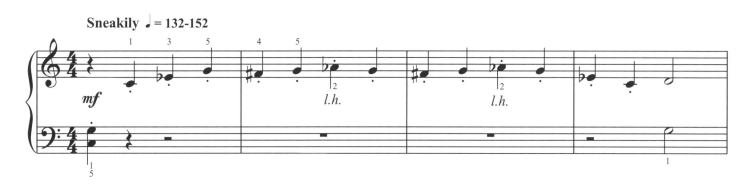

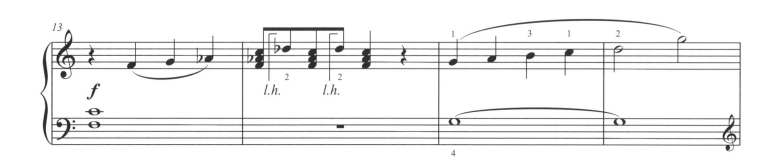

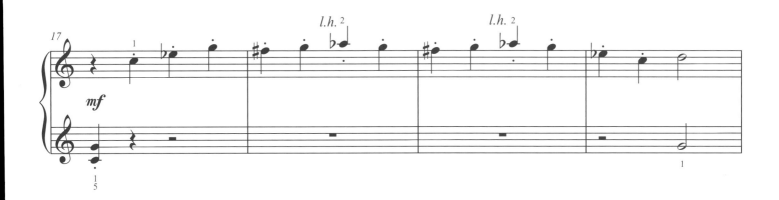

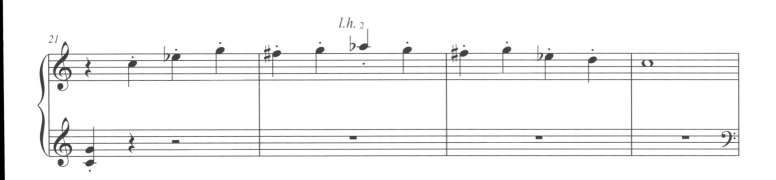

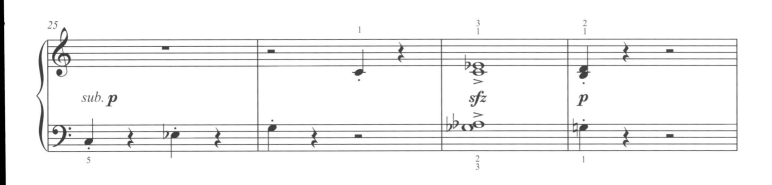

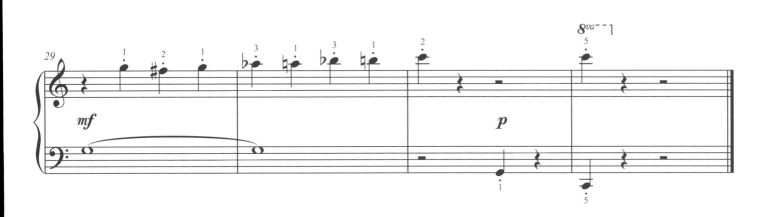

Pirate Stomp

Naomi Yandell
(b. 1961)

The Croc That Swallowed a Clock

Mark Tanner
(b. 1963)

(cluster chord!)

Space Walk Rag

Philip Hawthorn & Anya Suschitzky

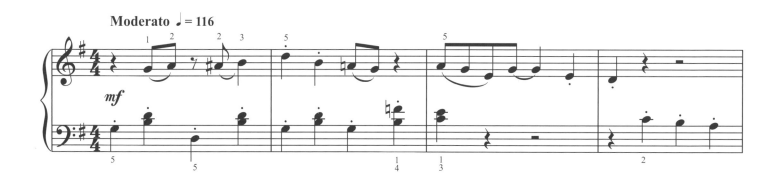

Reproduced from *The Usborne Book of Easy Piano Tunes*
by permission of Usborne Publishing, 83-85 Saffron Hill, London EC1N 8RT, UK
www.usborne.com. Copyright © 1989 Usborne Publishing Ltd.

The Very Vicious Velociraptor

Pauline Hall & Paul Drayton
(1924-2015/b. 1944)

from *Prehistoric Piano Time* by Pauline Hall © Oxford University Press 1996

Viking Village

Matthew Pittarello
(b. 2011)

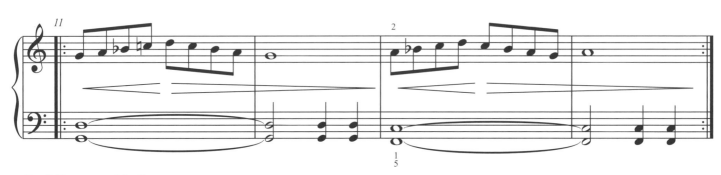

Omit the repeat in the exam.

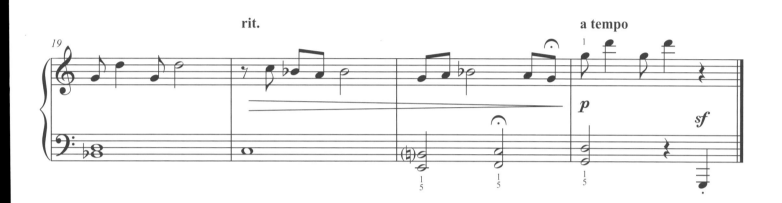

Exercises

1a. Sunny Afternoon – tone, balance and voicing

1b. Good Morning – tone, balance and voicing

2a. Walk and Whistle – co-ordination

2b. Country Estate – co-ordination

3a. Thoughtful Mood – finger & wrist strength and flexibility

3b. At the Market – finger & wrist strength and flexibility